Lenny the Lazy Puppy

"Don't worry, Lauren," Lenny woofed. "I'm going to find your jacket."

Lauren bent down and ruffled Lenny's ear, but she and Michelle and Mr Miller were busy deciding where to search for the jacket. They didn't see Lenny sniffing the grass carefully, then hurrying away, his nose glued to the ground . . .

Spot the Sporty Puppy

Suddenly Spot saw Matt. He was dressed in his sports kit and was standing on the opposite side of the track. Spot was so excited he dashed out from under the chair where he was hiding and across the track. At exactly the same moment the teachers came running at full speed towards him, Mr Brown still in the lead . . .

Spot had no time to get out of the way. Neither did the headmaster . . .

Jenny Dale's PUPPY TALES™ can be ordered from the Pan Macmillan website, www.panmacmillan.com, or from your local bookshop, and are also available by post from:

**Bookpost, PO Box 29, Douglas,
Isle of Man IM99 1BQ**
Tel: 01624 836000
Email: bookshop@enterprise.net
www.bookpost.co.uk

A Puppy Tales™
Two-Books-in-One Special!

Lenny the Lazy Puppy
Spot the Sporty Puppy

by Jenny Dale

Illustrated by Frank Rodgers

A Working Partners Book

MACMILLAN CHILDREN'S BOOKS

Lenny the Lazy Puppy and *Spot the Sporty Puppy* first published 1999
by Macmillan Children's Books

This edition first published 2004 by Macmillan Children's Books
a division of Macmillan Publishers Limited
20 New Wharf Road, London N1 9RR
Basingstoke and Oxford
www.panmacmillan.com

Associated companies throughout the world

Created by Working Partners Limited
London W6 0QT

ISBN 0 330 43506 X

1 3 5 7 9 8 6 4 2

A CIP catalogue record for this book is available from
the British Library.

Typeset by SX Composing DTP, Rayleigh, Essex
Printed and bound in Great Britain by Mackays of Chatham plc, Kent

Lenny the Lazy Puppy

With Special thanks to Narinder Dhami

Chapter One

"Come on, Lenny! Fetch!"
shouted Lauren. "Fetch the ball!"
She threw the ball up into the sky
in a wide arc, and it bounced
down onto the grass.

Lenny, who was lying in the
sun, opened one eye and yawned.
Then he closed it again.

"I thought he was supposed to be a retriever," said Lauren's best friend, Michelle.

"He is," Lauren replied with a grin.

"Well, that means he's supposed to run after things and bring them back, doesn't it?" Michelle pointed out.

Only when I want to, Lenny thought lazily. He yawned again. It was quite a long walk from the Millers' house to the park and now they'd arrived, he wanted to have a snooze. He didn't want to run up and down after a silly old ball. Besides, he knew that Lauren would run after it and bring it back anyway, if he didn't.

"He's *supposed* to retrieve

things, but he doesn't," said Mr Miller, Lauren's father. They were strolling along a broad path between some beautiful rose bushes. "I don't think I've ever seen a lazier puppy!"

What a cheek! Lenny thought indignantly. *I'm not lazy. I'm just saving my energy.*

"Come and play piggy in the middle, Dad," Lauren called, running back with the ball in her hand.

"Er . . . no, thanks, love," said Mr Miller quickly. "I'll just sit on that bench over there and read my newspaper."

Lenny sat up when he heard that. "And he says *I'm* lazy!" he barked.

Lauren went over and stroked her puppy's shaggy golden coat. "Sure you don't want to play, Lenny?"

Lenny licked her hand. He loved Lauren, but he really didn't want to run around and get all hot and out of breath. He wanted to snooze in the warm sun.

Lauren and Michelle ran off

together across the park and began throwing the ball to each other. They were quite a long way away from Lenny but he could just about hear what they were saying.

"I had a great time at your birthday party yesterday," Michelle called to Lauren.

So did I, Lenny thought dreamily. He had lain under the table all afternoon, waiting for bits of birthday party food to be dropped near him.

"I loved the present you bought me," Lauren called back.

Lenny opened one eye and woofed his agreement. Michelle had given Lauren a pencil case with pictures of puppies just like Lenny all over it.

"Have you decided what you're going to buy with the birthday money your gran and auntie sent you?" Michelle asked.

Lauren shook her head. "Not yet."

Lenny stopped listening to the two girls and began to doze off. The sun felt deliciously warm on his furry coat and the long grass underneath him was soft and springy. He stretched out his shaggy paws and settled down even more comfortably.

"Dad!" Just as he was drifting off to sleep, Lenny heard Lauren calling her father. "Dad! We've lost the ball in the bushes and we can't find it!"

Mr Miller looked over the top of

his newspaper. "Have you had a *good* look?" he asked.

"Yes, we have," Lauren told him. "But we can't see it anywhere."

"We could get Lenny to help us look for it," Michelle suggested.

"We'll be here all day if we do that!" Mr Miller answered, smiling. He folded his newspaper and stood up. "Come on, I'll give you a hand."

Good, Lenny thought happily. *Now I can have a nice snooze in peace and quiet.*

A few seconds later he was fast asleep, dreaming of big juicy bones . . .

"Dad! Dad!"

Lenny woke up suddenly.

"Oh, Lauren, what did you go and do a silly thing like that for?" Her father sighed and shook his head. "Someone must have taken it while we were looking for the ball."

Lenny whined and pawed at Lauren's leg. He wished now that he hadn't gone to sleep. Maybe then he would have seen what had happened to her jacket.

Lauren was calling again. He didn't know how long he'd been asleep but it could only have been a few minutes. He looked up to see Lauren and Michelle standing on the grass where they had been playing ball, looking very upset.

Lenny jumped to his feet and dashed over to the two girls. He couldn't bear it when Lauren was unhappy.

Mr Miller came out of the bushes. He had bits of leaves and twigs in his hair but he was clutching the ball triumphantly. "What's the matter, Lauren?"

"My – my jacket!" Lauren said tearfully. "I left it here on the grass while we were playing and now it's gone!"

"What did you have in the pockets?" Mr Miller went on. "Anything important?"

Now Lauren began to cry. "My birthday money!" she sobbed. "All my birthday money was in it!"

"Oh, *Lauren!*" said her father again, looking cross. "You should have given it to me to look after."

"Never mind, Lauren," Michelle said. She put an arm round her friend's shoulder. "Come on, we'll have a look around and see if we can find it."

Lenny felt very bad indeed. If he'd stayed awake and guarded Lauren's jacket, then it wouldn't have been taken. He slumped at Lauren's feet. "It's all my fault," he snuffled to himself.

Then Lenny sat up again. "I have to try to put things right," he told himself sternly. He licked Lauren's knee. "Don't worry, Lauren," he woofed. "I'm going to find your jacket."

Lauren bent down and ruffled Lenny's ear, but she and Michelle and Mr Miller were busy deciding where to search for the jacket. They didn't see Lenny sniffing the grass carefully, then hurrying away, his nose glued to the ground.

Lenny wasn't worried about going off on his own. He knew how to find his way back home from the park if he had to. The most important thing now was to find Lauren's jacket – and get her

birthday money back.

He was a retriever, wasn't he?
Well, now he was going to
retrieve that missing jacket!

Chapter Two

At first Lenny was confused –
there were so many smells around.
But his sharp nose soon picked up
Lauren's scent. As he began to
follow the trail, Lenny detected the
scents of two other people as well.
*They must be the ones who took the
jacket*, he thought indignantly.

Sniffing this way and that, Lenny followed the trail off the grass and onto the path. He went along quite slowly. There were so many smells that it was sometimes hard to pick out the one he was looking for. He trotted further and further down the winding path.

"It's not here!" Lauren said, beginning to cry again. She, Michelle and Mr Miller had searched every centimetre of the grass where they had been playing, and they'd even looked in the bushes. But there was no sign of her jacket.

"Someone might have picked it up and taken it to the park

keeper's office," Michelle suggested.

Mr Miller nodded. "That's a good idea," he said. "I'm sure the park keeper looks after lost property. We'd better go and try there."

"Where's Lenny?" Lauren asked suddenly, looking round. "Lenny! Lenny! Come here, boy!"

But there was no sign of her retriever puppy.

"Oh no!" Lauren cried. "Now we've lost Lenny as well!"

"He's probably asleep somewhere," Mr Miller said crossly. "We'll just have to keep calling him until he wakes up."

"Maybe he's gone to look for your jacket!" Michelle suggested brightly. "He is a *retriever*, after all!"

Mr Miller shook his head and smiled. "I don't think so," he replied. "That puppy couldn't retrieve a bone if it was put right under his nose!" He picked up his newspaper from the bench. "Come on, you two. Let's go and find the park keeper – we can look for Lenny on the way."

Lenny was concentrating so hard that he didn't hear the footsteps behind him. Then someone spoke.

"I don't like stray dogs running round my park, Danny," said a stern voice. "If you find one, just call the Dogs' Home – they'll

come and take it. Understand?
There are far too many strays
around here."

Lenny stopped in his tracks.
He knew that voice! It was Mr
Fraser, the park keeper. All the
dogs who came to the park were
scared of Mr Fraser. He was a
tall, fierce-looking man with a
little moustache, and he patrolled
the park with an eagle eye. He
didn't like litter, he didn't like
noisy children and he didn't like
dogs – especially stray dogs.

Lenny wasn't a stray, and he had
a tag on his collar with his name
and address on, but he didn't want
to take any chances. He dived into
a thick clump of bushes and
ducked down out of sight.

Mr Fraser marched down the path, still talking. He was with someone Lenny hadn't seen before – a bored-looking young man with dark brown hair and glasses.

"There's a lot to learn about being an assistant park keeper, Danny," Mr Fraser was saying.

"This is only your first day on the job, so make sure you keep your eyes and ears open."

"Yeah, OK," said Danny with a yawn.

"Yes, *Mr Fraser*, if you don't mind," snapped Mr Fraser, frowning crossly.

Lenny waited until the two men had gone by. Then he tried to jump out of the bushes. But he couldn't move – his collar had caught on a large twig!

Lenny struggled and strained, frantically trying to free himself. But it was no use – he was well and truly stuck. There was only one thing left to do. Pulling backwards really hard, he squeezed his head out of the

collar, leaving it hanging on the
bush.

He was free! But now that he
didn't have a collar and tag on,
he'd have to keep a sharp lookout
for the two park keepers . . .

Lenny hurried over to the path
again and sniffed around until he
picked up the trail. After a few
minutes it led him towards the

large lake in the middle of the park. Then, suddenly, the trail stopped.

Lenny's heart sank. He ran round frantically in circles, trying to pick up the scent again, but it was no good. There were just too many mixed-up smells for him to find the one he was looking for.

He wandered along the water's edge, still sniffing the ground.

There were lots of ducks on the lake, as well as two swans, which bobbed up and down in the water, hunting for leftover bits of bread. Lenny kept a wary eye on them. He'd chased the swans once before when he'd come to the park. One of them had given him a nasty nip with its strong

beak. He'd never done it again!

Lenny stopped sniffing and began to feel miserable. It looked as if he would have to go back to Lauren without finding her jacket after all. Some retriever he had turned out to be. He hadn't found *anything*.

Lenny yawned and lay down under a tree. He was feeling a bit tired. All that running around had worn him out. Maybe he'd just have a little rest before he started looking again . . .

"Hey, you!" shouted a loud, familiar voice which made Lenny quiver all over with fear. "Get away from the water and stop chasing those ducks!"

It was Mr Fraser, the park keeper!

Chapter Three

Lenny jumped to his feet. Mr
Fraser was racing towards him,
his face red with anger. His
assistant, Danny, was running
along behind him.

Lenny couldn't risk getting
caught, now that he didn't have
his collar on! He turned and ran

for his life. He raced away from the water's edge and back up the path. Mr Fraser and Danny were in hot pursuit.

"Come on, Danny, can't you run any faster?" grumbled Mr Fraser, as he lumbered along. "I want that dog caught – it's got no collar on – obviously a stray!"

"I'm – doing – my – best!" Danny wheezed, panting heavily.

"A young lad like you should be able to run faster than that!" Mr Fraser told him sternly. *"Aargh!* Get out of my way, you stupid creatures!"

The park keeper had to skid to a sudden halt as a crowd of ducks, and the two swans, waddled eagerly towards them, hoping to be fed.

Danny wasn't expecting Mr Fraser to stop quite so suddenly and he crashed into the back of the park keeper, almost sending Mr Fraser head first into the lake.

"Why don't you look where you're going?" roared Mr Fraser.

"It wasn't my fault!" Danny said indignantly. "You shouldn't have stopped like that!"

Mr Fraser glared at his new assistant. "I want that dog caught before it causes any damage in my park!" he bellowed. "Ow!" Mr Fraser jumped back as an angry swan nipped smartly at his ankle.

Lenny didn't stop running until he was a long way from the lake. Then he turned round and looked behind him. Mr Fraser and Danny were nowhere to be seen, thank goodness.

Lenny didn't know what to do. He was tired out and he'd lost the trail of Lauren's jacket. He'd never find it now.

He padded sadly down the path and back towards the place where Lauren and Michelle had been playing ball. He was looking forward to having his usual afternoon nap when they got home, but he really wished he'd been able to find Lauren's jacket.

While Lenny was busy running away from the park keepers, Lauren, Michelle and Mr Miller made their way to the office. It was a small, square wooden building which looked rather like a shed. It stood on the other side of the park, near the tennis courts.

"I hope someone's handed the jacket in," said Mr Miller as they walked along the path.

"So do I," Michelle added.

But Lauren wasn't listening. She

was looking around the park and frowning. "I'm more worried about Lenny," she said. "This is a big park – what if he really is lost?"

"Oh, I'm sure he's around here somewhere," Mr Miller replied as they stopped outside the office. "He's too lazy to go far. He'll come back if we shout loud enough."

"I don't think the park keeper's here," said Michelle.

Mr Miller knocked on the door, but no one answered. Then he tried the handle, but the door was locked. Mr Miller looked through the window. There was no sign of Lauren's jacket inside the small office.

"What are we going to do now?" Michelle asked, looking worried.

"I want to go and find Lenny," Lauren said firmly. "He might be getting scared all on his own."

Mr Miller smiled. "I expect he's asleep somewhere, safe and sound."

"I don't care," Lauren said stubbornly. "I don't care about

my jacket or my birthday money, as long as I get Lenny back!"

"Come on, then," said Mr Miller with a sigh. "We'd better go and look for him . . ."

Lenny arrived back at the place where Lauren's jacket had gone missing. He was feeling so tired he could hardly put one paw in front of the other. He couldn't wait to get home.

But there was no sign of Lauren, Michelle or Mr Miller. Lenny wondered where they were. He was sure Lauren wouldn't have gone home without him. They must be somewhere in the park.

He sniffed around until he picked up their trail and, nose to the ground again, he began to follow it.

The scent led him back to the path, then in the opposite direction, away from the lake. Lenny was glad. He didn't want to meet Mr Fraser and Danny again!

Lenny trotted on for a while, concentrating hard. But suddenly he picked up another scent. He stopped, feeling very excited. "That's the two people I followed before!" Lenny snuffled to himself. And the scent was getting stronger and stronger . . .

Lenny raised his head and saw two boys coming down the path towards him. They were arguing at the tops of their voices and one of them was carrying something over his arm. Lenny recognised it straight away. It was Lauren's jacket!

Chapter Four

Lenny stared angrily at the two boys as they came nearer. Had they *stolen* Lauren's jacket?

Lenny began to growl softly, deep in his throat. If they had, they were in for a surprise!

"I thought you said you knew where the park keeper's office

was, Jamie!" the smallest of the two boys grumbled as they came nearer. "We've been walking around for ages now – Mum's going to be mad at us for being late!"

"Well, we can't just leave the jacket here, can we, Ben?" said Jamie. "Someone might be looking for it."

Lenny stopped growling. It sounded as if the two boys had found Lauren's jacket lying on the grass and decided to hand it in at the office. But they must have lost their way.

"Let's take it home with us," suggested Ben. "Mum will know what to do."

Lenny whimpered softly. If the

two boys took the jacket home with them, Lauren might *never* get it back! There was only one thing to do. He padded down the path to meet the two boys.

"Look, Jamie." Ben nudged his brother. "See that puppy?"

"He looks a bit young to be out on his own, doesn't he?" Jamie knelt down and held out his hand to Lenny. "Good boy! Come here!"

Lenny rushed over to him. But instead of letting Jamie stroke him he grabbed the sleeve of Lauren's jacket in his teeth and pulled hard.

"Hey, what are you doing?" Jamie laughed. He tried to tug the sleeve gently out of Lenny's mouth but the puppy wouldn't let go.

"Maybe he knows who it belongs

to," Ben suggested with a grin.

"Don't be daft!" Jamie tugged
at the jacket again but Lenny
clung on. "Come and help me get
it off him."

Lenny began to feel nervous. He
wasn't sure if he could hold on to
the coat with both boys pulling at
it. He did the only thing he could
think of: he gave a fierce growl.

"Did you hear that?" Ben stopped and looked at Jamie. "He's dangerous!"

"He's just playing," Jamie replied, but he looked a bit scared himself.

"Well, his tail's not wagging!" Ben pointed out.

Lenny growled again, as fiercely as he could. This time Jamie dropped the jacket on the ground and backed away, closely followed by his brother.

"All right, all right, we're going!" he told Lenny. "You can *have* the jacket!"

The two boys ran off. Lenny barked happily. He'd done it! He'd got the jacket back. Now he was a real retriever!

Lenny was so proud of himself he felt he might burst! He couldn't wait to hear what Lauren, Michelle and Mr Miller would say – *especially* Mr Miller. They wouldn't be able to call him lazy any more!

Lenny pushed his nose into the pocket of the jacket. Lauren's purse was still inside, thank goodness! He tried to lift the jacket off the ground but it was too heavy.

He'd have to drag it along, he decided. The jacket would get a bit dirty, but Lenny didn't think Lauren would mind. After all, she was going to get her birthday money back – thanks to him!

Dragging the jacket was such hard work that Lenny didn't

notice two tall shadows creeping through the trees towards him. It was not until the very last moment that he saw one of the shadows coming up behind him. And by then it was too late . . .

A hand shot out and firmly grabbed the scruff of Lenny's neck. Lenny howled and tried to wriggle free, but he couldn't.

"Got him!"

"Well done, Danny!" said Mr Fraser, hurrying to join the assistant park keeper. "Now don't let go!"

"I won't," Danny said importantly. "What do we do now, Mr Fraser?"

The park keeper frowned at Lenny. "He's not wearing a collar

and identity tag, so he must be a stray. We'll have to send him to the Dogs' Home."

Lenny cowered behind Danny's legs, feeling very frightened. "I don't want to go to the Dogs' Home," he whimpered. "I've got a proper home – with Lauren!"

"Right!" said Mr Fraser. "Let's go back to the office and we'll phone the Dogs' Home and ask them to come and collect him."

Lenny began to shake with fear. Everything had gone wrong, and now he was in big trouble. If he was taken to the Dogs' Home, he might never see Lauren again!

Chapter Five

Lenny looked up at Danny and
whined unhappily.

Danny took no notice. "I
wonder where that came from?"
he said, pointing at Lauren's
jacket.

Mr Fraser picked it up.
"Someone must have lost it," he

43

said. "We'll take it back to the office and it can go into the lost property box."

Lenny watched Mr Fraser reach over to pick up the jacket. The puppy had been *so close* to retrieving Lauren's birthday money – and now she would never know. It just wasn't fair! Lenny was so cross, he couldn't help giving a little growl.

Mr Fraser dropped the jacket and leapt backwards as if he'd been stung by a bee. "That dog growled at me!" he said, glaring at Lenny.

Danny shrugged. "I didn't hear anything."

Mr Fraser stared hard at Lenny and shook his head. "You can

pick the jacket up, Danny," he muttered.

"What?" Danny said. "I thought I was supposed to be holding the dog!"

"Well, you can pick the jacket up too, can't you?" Mr Fraser snapped.

Danny looked annoyed. "OK, you hold the dog and I'll get the jacket." Danny began to drag Lenny nearer the park keeper.

"Er . . . no!" cried Mr Fraser, backing away. "No, you keep hold of him," he said.

Lenny noticed that the park keeper didn't look at all scary now. In fact, he looked *scared*! In a flash, Lenny realised something very interesting . . .

Mr Fraser was frightened of him!

"Look, make your mind up,
Mr Fraser," Danny said rudely. "Do
you want me to get the jacket or
do you want me to hold the dog?"

Before the park keeper could
reply, Lenny tried another growl
– a big, deep, fierce one this time.

Mr Fraser turned even paler,
and this time Danny looked a bit
nervous too.

"He's starting to get angry,"
Danny said, looking worried.
"What shall I do?"

"You're not frightened of a
young pup like that, are you?"
said Mr Fraser in a shaky voice.
The park keeper was pretending
not to be scared, but Lenny knew
better.

Lenny decided to help things along by growling loudly again and pretending to nip Danny's leg. Danny gave a howl of alarm and let go of Lenny.

Gleefully, Lenny rushed towards the terrified Mr Fraser.

"You idiot, Danny!" Mr Fraser roared. "He'll attack me now!" The park keeper tried to run, but tripped and fell over. *"Argh!"* he cried as the puppy bounded towards him.

At the last second, Lenny swerved past the quivering Mr Fraser and pounced on Lauren's jacket. He wasn't going to let them take it – and he wasn't going to let them send him to the Dogs' Home!

"Do something, Danny!" shouted Mr Fraser, who had now leapt up and taken cover behind a nearby tree.

Danny hesitated. Then he slipped off his coat and, holding it out in front of him, started to walk slowly towards Lenny. "Come on, boy," he said softly. "Good dog. Now keep still, you stupid mutt . . ."

Lenny growled indignantly, but Danny kept on coming towards him. Lenny knew that the man was going to grab him, but how could he run away? He had to stay and guard Lauren's jacket! Lenny braced himself . . .

Chapter Six

"What on earth's going on here?"

With a whimper of relief, Lenny recognised Mr Miller's deep voice.

Danny stopped in his tracks. *"Lenny!"*

Lenny knew that voice, too. It was the one he loved most in the whole world – Lauren's!

He turned round and barked joyfully. There were Lauren and Mr Miller and Michelle. Thank goodness!

Lauren dashed down the path and scooped her puppy into her arms. Lenny wriggled happily, trying to lick Lauren's face while she kissed the top of his head.

Mr Miller looked at Danny, who was still holding his coat out ready to trap Lenny. Then he looked over at Mr Fraser, who was still behind the tree. "What's up? Is everything all right?" he asked.

Before anyone could answer, Lauren spotted her jacket lying on the ground. "There it is!" she gasped.

"So this jacket's yours then, Miss?" Danny asked her. Lauren nodded. "And the dog too?"

Lauren nodded again and hugged Lenny closer.

"We thought he was a stray," Mr Fraser said, coming out from behind the tree. "Why hasn't he got a collar on?"

"He *did* have one," Lauren replied, looking at Lenny's neck. "He must have lost it."

Lenny licked Lauren's chin to show he agreed.

"You see, I lost my jacket," Lauren explained. "And while we were looking for it, Lenny went missing too. Then I didn't care about the jacket – I just wanted my puppy back."

Lenny's heart swelled with love. Lauren cared about him as much as he cared about her.

"The pup had the jacket when we caught him," Mr Fraser explained. "We don't know where he got it from."

"Hang on a minute," said Mr Miller, looking surprised. "Are

you telling us that *Lenny* found this jacket?"

Mr Fraser and Danny looked at each other, then nodded.

"Lenny!" cried Lauren, delighted. "You clever boy! I *knew* you could do it!"

Lenny's tail wagged madly.

"You're a hero, Lenny!" said Michelle, scratching the puppy's ears.

Lenny woofed his thanks.

Mr Miller smiled. "I thought you were far too lazy to be a good retriever, Lenny. But I take it all back! Well done!"

Lenny barked and wagged his tail again. He could get used to all this praise!

"We were going to take the

jacket to our office, weren't we,
Mr Fraser?" Danny said with a
grin. "But the pup didn't want
us to. And then when he
started growling, Mr Fraser got
scared—"

"That's enough, thank you,
Danny," said Mr Fraser hurriedly.

"Oh, but Lenny's really
friendly!" Lauren said, carrying
the puppy up to the park keeper.
"Look, you can stroke him if
you like!"

Mr Fraser looked as if he'd rather
pet a man-eating tiger, but he put
out a cautious hand and touched
the top of the puppy's head.

Lenny gave a little woof, and
Mr Fraser jumped back, looking
alarmed.

"He's just saying hello!" Lauren grinned.

Mr Fraser smiled weakly and gave Lenny another little pat.

Lenny wagged his tail madly. He couldn't *wait* to tell the other dogs he met in the park that he'd just made friends with the fearsome Mr Fraser!

"I think we'd better go home,"

Mr Miller said with a grin as Lenny yawned widely. "I think Lenny needs a nap – all that excitement must have tired him out!"

"It has!" Lenny woofed, yawning again.

"I'll carry you home, boy," said Lauren.

They said goodbye to Danny and Mr Fraser and set off for home.

Lenny snuggled down happily in Lauren's arms. He was going to enjoy coming to the park much more now that he wasn't scared of Mr Fraser.

"See, Dad?" said Lauren as they walked towards the park gates. "Lenny *did* find my jacket!"

"Yes, Lenny did very well," Mr Miller replied. "I thought he was too lazy to be a proper retriever, but he proved me wrong."

"Yes, I did," Lenny woofed proudly . . .

. . . and then he fell asleep.

Spot the Sporty Puppy

To Reba – another sporty puppy!

With special thanks to Narinder Dhami

Chapter One

"Fetch the ball, Spot!"

Spot went chasing across the field. He grabbed the squeaky ball in his teeth and raced back to Matt. The ball made a dreadful noise as he ran.

"Good boy, Spot!" Matt, Spot's

owner, knelt down and stroked his Dalmatian puppy's silky black ears. "You're a really fast runner!"

Spot wagged his tail proudly and licked Matt's hand. Spot loved running nearly as much as he loved Matt. He would put his ears back and race from one end of the field to the other, feeling the wind rushing past him and ruffling his fur. It was better than a big, juicy bone, or even a roll in a dirty puddle.

Matt looked at his watch. "Time to go home, Spot, or I'm going to be late for school."

Spot whined grumpily. He didn't want to go home yet. Every morning Matt took him for a long walk in the playing field behind their house, where Spot met up with some of the other dogs that lived in their street. They usually had races and Spot, of course, always won. But this morning Matt seemed in a hurry.

"Sorry, Spot," Matt said, as he clipped the lead to his puppy's collar. "I promise I'll take you out for a longer walk tonight."

Spot woofed. He didn't really mind going home because he had a special secret. A *very* special secret. When Matt was at school and Mrs Robinson, Matt's mum, was at work, Spot could run around the field as much as he liked!

Matt and Spot went across the field to the Robinsons' back gate.

Matt opened it and then closed

it carefully behind them. "Come on, Spot! Race you to the kitchen!"

Spot dashed up the garden path, his white tail wagging furiously from side to side, and got to the open kitchen door just before Matt did. He dived into the kitchen and skidded across the floor, stopping with expert

timing in front of his empty bowl.

"You're just in time for breakfast, Spot!" laughed Mrs Robinson, who was spreading butter on toast. She shook some dog biscuits into the bowl and Spot began to crunch them noisily.

"You won, Spot!" Matt said with a grin. "Mum, did you wash my kit ready for Sports Day this afternoon?"

Spot stopped eating and pricked up his ears. Did Matt say *Spot's* Day?

Matt saw Spot looking eagerly up at him and smiled. "No, not *Spot's* Day – *Sports* Day!"

Spot didn't know what Sports Day was, so he wasn't very interested. He went back to eating his biscuits.

"You *are* coming to watch, aren't you, Mum?" Matt asked.

Mrs Robinson nodded. "I'll be home from work at lunchtime, so I'll be there to cheer you on."

"Great!" said Matt. "I'm going to try really hard to win one of the races this year!"

Spot's ears pricked up again when he heard the word *race*. He still didn't know what Sports Day was, but he was beginning to like the sound of it! He hoped that he would be allowed to go this afternoon too.

"Time to go, Matt," said Mrs Robinson.

Spot dashed over to the kitchen door, and barked.

"Do you want to stay in the garden this morning, Spot?" asked Mrs Robinson with a smile.

Spot barked again, so she carried the puppy's bowls outside and gave him some more biscuits and some fresh water. "Matt, you did shut the back gate properly, didn't you?" she asked. "We don't want Spot getting out."

Matt nodded. "Bye, Spot. See you later."

Spot waited until he heard the car start up and drive away, taking Mrs Robinson to work and Matt to school. Then he scampered eagerly to the other end of the garden. He scrabbled about at the bottom of the hedge and uncovered his secret – a small hole. He squeezed his way through, and then he was out in the playing field again.

Spot ran joyfully across the grass, sniffing the air as he went. He knew he wasn't really allowed out on his own, but he got so bored at home when Matt was at school. This way he could meet up with all his other friends!

He ran about on his own for a while, scrabbling in the hedgerows and finding lots of interesting smells. Then he saw Jasper the black Labrador, who lived a few doors away from the Robinsons. Jasper was out with his owner, Mr Smith.

Spot bounded up to him and gave him a friendly nudge with

his nose. "Come on, I'll race you to the other end of the field!" he barked.

"Oh no, not again!" Jasper groaned. "You always beat me!"

"Hello, Spot." Mr Smith bent down and patted the Dalmatian. "You're out on your own again, I see!"

Spot woofed and wagged his tail. He hoped Mr Smith wouldn't

say anything to the Robinsons, or his special secret would be discovered!

Spot and Jasper set off across the field. Spot was soon in front and he won the race easily, before Jasper had even run halfway. The Labrador gave up, panting.

"You shouldn't eat so many biscuits!" Spot yapped at him. "Then you'd be able to run as fast as me!"

Jasper lay down and put his nose between his paws. "I need a rest!" he whined.

Spot suddenly thought of something. "Jasper, do you know what *Sports Day* is?"

"It's a special day for children at school," Jasper woofed back.

"They have lots of races, and all the mums and dads go to watch."

Spot's eyes lit up. A moment later he was running away across the field again.

"Where are you going?" Jasper barked after him.

"Home!" Spot barked back. "I don't want to miss Sports Day!"

It seemed a very long time to Spot before Mrs Robinson arrived home at lunchtime. He jumped around, whining impatiently, as she opened the back door.

"Hello, Spot!" She patted him, then checked that he still had water in his bowl. "I've got to rush – I'm late for Sports Day!"

Spot began to bark at the top of

his voice, feeling very excited.
He could hardly wait to go and
join in all the races!

"No, you can't come, I'm afraid,
Spot," said Matt's mum, and she
quickly locked the back door again.

Spot slumped miserably on the
grass. *Why* couldn't he go to
Sports Day? After all, he was the
fastest dog in the street! If there
were races going on, he ought to
be allowed to take part in them . . .

Spot's ears pricked up. He
could hear voices. Lots of them.
It sounded as if there were
suddenly lots of people in the
playing field.

He hurried down to the end of
the garden and looked through
his secret hole in the hedge.

There *were* lots of people in
the field. And there were some
strange, exciting things happening
too. Balloons and streamers had
been tied up in the trees. There
were lots of chairs laid out in
rows, as well as a small platform
with people standing on it.

Spot was puzzled. Who were all
these people, and what was going

on?

Then, to his delight, Spot saw Matt! The puppy could hardly believe his eyes. So *this* must be Sports Day! And it was happening right there, in his own playing field! Spot only had to squeeze through the secret hole to go and join in the fun. And that was just what he was going to do!

Chapter Two

Spot was so excited it took him a
moment or two to wriggle his
way through the hole in the
hedge. But at last, he did it. He
raced happily across the field
towards the crowd of people,
hoping he hadn't missed any of
the races. But nothing much

seemed to be happening, except that a man was standing on the little platform, talking to the parents and children who sat in rows on either side of him.

". . . And as headmaster of Redhill Primary School, it gives me great pleasure to welcome all of you here to Sports Day," the man was saying. "We'll start with the special teachers' race. All the teachers will be taking part, including myself!"

Spot had heard Matt talking about the headmaster. His name was Mr Brown and Matt was a bit scared of him because he was very strict. As people clapped the headmaster's speech, Spot bared his teeth and growled a little. He hoped Mr Brown didn't win!

Nobody noticed the puppy as he looked around for Matt. The teachers were lining up at the top of the track for the start of the race. There were two children standing at the bottom end, holding a tape stretched out between them. That was the finishing-line.

Spot felt very excited. How wonderful it would feel to be the first to cross the line and win! All these people would jump up and cheer, and Matt would be very proud of him . . .

"Spot! What on earth are *you* doing here?"

Spot's heart sank. Mrs Robinson had seen him! She had jumped up from her seat and was hurrying across the grass towards him. She didn't look very pleased, either.

Spot knew very well that if he was caught he'd be taken home again, so he scurried off as fast as his legs could carry him.

"Spot, you naughty boy!" Mrs Robinson called. "Come back!"

Spot pretended he hadn't heard. He decided to find a place to hide and wriggled under a row of chairs, squeezing his way around people's legs.

Some of the people leant down and tried to grab him as he rushed by. But Spot managed to wriggle away from them.

Just then, Mrs Williams, the school secretary, shouted, "On your marks! Get set! *Go!*"

The teachers' race had started!
Spot crawled forward to sit under
a chair in the front row, right next
to the track. He poked his head
out to see what was going on.

The teachers were all charging
across the grass towards the
finishing-line. Mr Brown was in
the lead and he looked determined
to win.

Spot wondered if the other

teachers were letting Mr Brown win because he was the head-master. He wished *he* had a chance to race against Mr Brown – he was sure he could beat him.

"Spot!"

That was Matt's voice. Spot sat up eagerly and looked around.

"Spot!"

Then Spot saw his owner. Matt was dressed in his sports kit and was standing on the opposite side of the track with his best friend, Daniel Parsons.

Spot was so excited he dashed out from under the chair where he was hiding and across the track. At exactly the same moment the teachers came running at full speed towards him, Mr Brown still in the lead.

Spot had no time to get out of the way. Neither did the headmaster. They crashed into each other with a yelp and a shout. Mr Brown tripped over Spot and went flying head over heels, landing in a heap on the grass!

Chapter Three

"What . . . who . . . ?" spluttered
Mr Brown in a dazed voice, as he
pulled himself to his feet. "What is
this . . . this *animal* doing here?"

Spot cowered in the grass,
feeling very frightened. He hadn't
meant to trip up Mr Brown. The
headmaster looked very big and

menacing as he towered over Spot. The puppy was glad when Matt rushed over and picked him up.

"Sorry, sir," Matt said breathlessly. "He's mine."

"And what's he doing at Sports Day?" Mr Brown glared down at Spot, who huddled even closer to Matt. "No dogs are allowed!"

"He must have got out of our back garden somehow," Matt explained quickly. "We live just there." He pointed to his house.

Mr Brown opened his mouth to say something else, then changed his mind. He'd noticed that some of the children and their parents were laughing, and even the teachers who'd now finished the race were trying not to smile.

"Well, get rid of him then," he snapped. "And quickly!"

Spot whimpered as Matt hurried across the track towards his mum. The parents and children who were watching were still laughing and pointing at them. Spot felt very ashamed of himself.

"It's OK, Spot," Matt whispered quietly into his puppy's ear. "Thanks to you, my teacher Miss Marshall won the race!"

Spot looked up at Matt and gave him a grateful lick on the chin. He felt a bit better now. Then Spot saw the look on Mrs Robinson's face . . .

"You're a very bad boy, Spot!" she scolded as Matt handed the

puppy to her. "You could have
caused a serious accident!"

Spot whimpered anxiously and
tried to lick her hand.

"This is your fault as well,
Matt," Mrs Robinson went on.
"You can't have closed the back
gate properly this morning, and
Spot must have got out."

Spot felt terrible when he heard
that. He didn't want Matt to be

blamed when it wasn't his fault. He began to whine loudly, but stopped as he saw Mr Brown glaring at him again.

"I'd better take Spot home right away," Mrs Robinson sighed, "before he can do any more damage!"

Matt's face fell. "But if you go now, you'll miss my first race!" he said. "It's the egg and spoon."

Mrs Robinson hesitated. "Well, all right. I'll stay and watch that first."

Spot's tail began to wag a little. At least he was going to see Matt take part in *one* race!

"You'd better behave yourself now, Spot," Mrs Robinson said firmly, as she sat down with the puppy on her lap. "I think Mr Brown's had enough of you for one day!"

"Hello, Spot!" said the woman who was sitting next to Mrs Robinson.

Spot knew who she was and wagged his tail. It was Mrs Parsons, Daniel's mum, and she had Daniel's little sister Emma in her arms.

"Dog!" said Emma, trying to grab Spot's ear. "Dog! Woof, woof!"

Spot licked her hand, and Emma squealed with delight.

"Look, Emma," said Mrs Parsons, lifting the little girl up. "There's Daniel and Matt!"

Spot looked up the track too, and saw Matt and his friend lining up for the egg and spoon race. Spot wasn't sure what an egg and spoon race was. Did the children have to eat the egg with the spoon?

"On your marks!" shouted Mr Brown, who was starting off the race.

Spot was amazed to see that all the children, including Matt, were holding a spoon with an egg balanced on it.

"Get set!" shouted Mr Brown. "*Go!*"

The race began. The children set off, half-running and half-walking, carefully holding their eggs and spoons in front of them.

Spot watched, puzzled. What a strange race! But he began to get excited when he saw that

Matt was in the lead!

"Come on, Matt!" shouted Mrs Robinson, bouncing Spot up and down on her knee.

Spot barked loudly, straining forward to get a better view. Matt was still in the lead, running along very carefully, his eyes fixed on the egg in front of him.

But then, just as Matt drew level with Mrs Robinson and Spot, he stumbled. The egg fell off his spoon into the grass.

Matt's mum had got so excited watching the race that she'd loosened her grip on Spot. Spot didn't hesitate. He leapt off her lap and dashed across the grass to pick up the egg. If he took it to the finishing-line, Matt might still win!

The other children taking part in the race were so surprised to see Spot darting in front of them that they all dropped their eggs too. Spot ignored them and grabbed Matt's egg in his teeth.

The egg was surprisingly hard and shiny. It felt more like a stone or a pebble. Spot decided it couldn't be a real egg, after all.

"Spot!" Matt was running towards him. "Come here!"

Spot galloped off towards the finishing-line, making sure that Matt was following him. He dashed under the tape and was thrilled to hear cheers from the crowd.

Matt followed him a few seconds later. They'd won! Spot danced

around Matt's ankles, barking loudly with delight.

"This dog is ruining our Sports Day!" boomed an angry voice.

Everyone fell silent as Mr Brown, panting and red in the face, hurried down the track towards Matt and Spot.

Alarmed, Spot hid behind Matt's legs, trying to make himself as small as possible. He'd done the wrong thing *again*. But he'd only wanted to help Matt win a race!

"I'm terribly sorry, Mr Brown," said Mrs Robinson, as she rushed over and picked Spot up. "I'll take him home right away."

"Thank you," snapped the headmaster. "I think we'd better

run the race again – and this time we'll do it properly!"

Spot looked miserably over Mrs Robinson's shoulder as she carried him away from all the fun. He'd got Matt into trouble again, and they hadn't even won the race in the end. It looked as if Sports Day was over for Spot.

Chapter Four

"In you go, Spot." Mrs Robinson swung open the back gate and took the puppy inside the garden. She frowned. "Why wasn't the gate still open? Oh, well, the wind must have blown it shut after you'd got out."

She wagged her finger sternly at

Spot. "Now you behave yourself
until we get back!"

Spot sat on the grass and looked
up at Mrs Robinson, his brown
eyes miserable.

Mrs Robinson couldn't help
smiling. "It's all right, Spot," she
said, giving him a pat. "I know
you didn't mean any harm. Be a

good boy, now. We'll be home soon."

She went out again, checking the gate to make sure it was properly shut.

Gloomily, Spot lay down and put his nose between his paws. He'd really made a mess of things this time. He'd got Matt into trouble with his mum *and* with his headmaster.

Suddenly the people in the field started cheering loudly. Spot couldn't help himself. He dashed straight over to his secret hole to see what was going on. But he was too far away to see anything much.

Everyone at Sports Day was having fun except him and it

didn't seem at all fair that he was left out.

Spot made up his mind and wriggled through the hole again. This time, he'd keep out of sight. He'd find a quiet hiding place where he could watch the races without being seen.

He crept cautiously across the field, keeping a sharp lookout. Some of the smallest children in the school were having a sack race, and they were all getting tangled up in their sacks and falling over. Everyone was watching the race so no one noticed Spot at all.

On the grass was a pile of sacks that weren't being used. Spot crawled towards them on his tummy and quickly burrowed his way underneath them.

He lay still for a moment or two, then carefully poked his head out and looked around. He soon dived back under the sacks again, though, because the first thing he saw was Mr Brown's shoes. The headmaster was standing right next to him!

"Class 3M! Skipping race next!" shouted Mr Brown loudly.

Spot knew that Matt was in Class 3M, so he risked a quick look out from under the sacks again. Luckily Mr Brown had walked over to the starting-line.

Spot had quite a good view, and he was thrilled to see Matt and Daniel lining up next to each other with skipping ropes. He longed to

bark loudly to encourage Matt, but he didn't dare.

"On your marks!" Mr Brown boomed, as the entrants stood holding their skipping ropes ready. Spot could hardly sit still because he was so excited.

"Get set!"

It was then that Spot noticed little Emma Parsons, Daniel's

sister, in the distance. She was toddling along on her own across the field, stopping now and then to pick a daisy.

Spot could see that Emma's mum was talking to Mrs Robinson. She'd probably put Emma down for a minute and not noticed that she'd wandered off, Spot decided.

Then Spot noticed something else: Emma was heading towards the open gateway at the top of the field.

Spot knew that beyond the gate was a very busy and dangerous road. Out on his lead with Matt, Spot had seen all sorts of huge scary lorries and buses on that road. Fast cars raced along it too. Spot was sure that little Emma shouldn't go near the road on her own.

"*Go!*" shouted Mr Brown.

At the same moment Spot leapt to his feet and rushed out from under the pile of sacks. He had to stop Emma from going through the gate. But would he make it in time?

Chapter Five

Spot took the quickest route towards Emma – which was straight across the track.

"It's that pest of a dog again!" roared Mr Brown furiously as Spot suddenly appeared and dashed in front of the skipping children. All of them, including

Matt, had to stop quickly, and most of them tripped on their skipping ropes and fell.

"Spot!" yelled Matt, trying to untangle himself from his rope. "Spot, come here!"

Spot took no notice. He knew he was a fast runner, but this was the fastest he had ever run in his life.

"Matthew Robinson! Will you get that dog of yours under control!" Mr Brown was shouting at the top of his voice as he dashed down the track. "I've had just about enough of this!"

"I'm trying, sir!" gasped Matt, who was still trying to untangle himself.

"I want that dog caught and taken away immediately—

Aaargh!" Mr Brown tripped over a trailing skipping rope and fell flat on his face.

"Are you all right, Mr Brown?" asked Mrs Robinson, who had hurried out from the audience to help.

"Yes, yes, never mind me!" Mr Brown muttered furiously as he struggled to his feet. "Just catch that dog!"

"Spot!" shouted Mrs Robinson. "Come back, right now!"

Spot ignored all the noise behind him and kept going, his eyes fixed firmly on Emma. Suddenly the field seemed very big and very long – and every second was taking Emma closer to the open gate and dangerous road beyond it. Spot wasn't sure he could get there in time, but he knew he had to try.

"Spot!" Matt was racing along behind him, followed by Mrs Robinson, Mr Brown and some of the other teachers who had joined in the chase. "Spot, will you *please* come back?"

Just then, Daniel Parsons noticed something. "Look, Mum!" he shouted. "Isn't that Emma heading towards the gate?"

"Oh my goodness, so it is!" gasped Mrs Parsons, her face turning pale. "She must have wandered off!" Mrs Parsons and Daniel leapt up and ran after the others.

Mr Brown had noticed Emma too and had forgotten about being angry with Spot. "Quick!" he shouted. "That child is heading towards the open gate. She'll be out on the main road any minute!"

"But look, Spot's trying to stop her!" Matt shouted in an excited voice. "Go on, Spot! Good boy! You can do it, I know you can!"

Spot heard Matt's shout from behind him and forced himself to run even faster. His legs were so tired, but Emma was almost at the open gate. Spot knew he had to make an extra big effort now to reach the toddler and somehow stop her going through it.

Yes! Spot leapt past Emma and swerved to a stop in front of her, making her stop too. By now they were right next to the gate. The sound of lorries and cars racing along outside was deafening.

"Dog!" said Emma happily, having no idea she had been in such danger. She patted the puppy. "Spot!"

Spot barked weakly. He felt as if he had no breath left. He'd just run the most important race of his life – and he'd won!

Chapter Six

"Good boy, Spot!" Matt reached Spot and Emma first. He picked his puppy up and hugged him.

Mrs Parsons was right behind Matt. She grabbed Emma and gave her a big hug too. "You shouldn't have gone off like that, Emma!" she said tearfully. "But thanks to Spot, you're safe!"

"Spot's a hero!" Daniel added as they walked back to the race track. All the children and parents and teachers cheered the puppy.

Only Mr Brown stayed silent. "Er . . . well," he muttered, as everyone turned to look at him. "I think that er . . . Spot . . . has done very well. Very well indeed . . . And he's welcome to stay and watch the rest of Sports Day . . ."

Everyone cheered and pretended not to hear when Mr Brown added, ". . . if he promises to behave himself!"

Spot barked loudly with delight, wagging his tail. He even thought about leaning over to lick Mr Brown's hand, but he decided against it. Spot still found the headmaster a bit scary!

Everyone sat down, ready to continue with Sports Day. Mrs Parsons kept a tight hold of Emma's hand.

Mr Brown announced that they would hold Class 3M's skipping race again, so Matt had to hurry off.

"I'm really proud of you, Spot!" he whispered in Spot's ear before he handed the puppy over to Mrs Robinson. "You showed Mr Brown just what a brilliant dog you are!"

Spot's heart swelled with pride. He sat on Mrs Robinson's knee to watch the skipping race, hoping that Matt would win.

Sadly, Matt and Daniel got tangled up in each other's ropes and they both came in last. Spot was a bit disappointed but this time he didn't try to interfere and stayed quietly on Mrs Robinson's lap.

It was great fun watching all the different races, and Spot barked loudly through all of them, even the ones Matt wasn't in.

The running race came last, and Spot thought that Matt had a good chance of winning. He sat forward eagerly as children from Class 3M lined up at the top of the track.

Matt waved at him. "I'm going to try to run as fast as you, Spot!" he called.

Spot barked his support then turned round and licked Mrs Robinson's chin excitedly.

Mr Brown got ready to start the race. "On your marks! Get set! *Go!*" he shouted.

Matt and the others started running. Spot was dismayed to see that at first a tall girl with very long legs was in the lead, but then he saw that Matt was catching up with her.

"Go on, Matt!" he barked. "You can do it!"

Matt heard Spot barking and that made him run even faster. He passed the girl and crossed the finishing-line – first!

Mrs Robinson was almost as excited as Spot, and she jumped up

and down with the puppy in her arms. "He won, Spot! He won!"

Spot was so proud he couldn't stop barking. He had been hoping and hoping that Matt would come first in a race, and now he had!

When the last race was over, it was time for Mr Brown to present certificates to the winners. Their names were called out one by one, and each winner went up onto the platform to shake hands with the headmaster.

Spot waited impatiently for Matt's turn. When Matt went up on that platform, Spot was going to bark louder than he'd ever barked in his life!

"And now the Class 3M running race," Mr Brown announced. Spot's tail began to wag furiously. "Our winner is . . . Matthew Robinson!"

Everyone clapped as Matt went up onto the platform, but they laughed too, because Spot was barking madly.

Mr Brown gave Matt his certificate, then he turned to the audience. "Sports Day is almost over now, but I have one very special presentation to make before we all go home."

Everyone sat up, wondering what was about to happen.

"We have a very clever dog here today," Mr Brown went on. "And after a few . . . er . . . hiccups . . . he has helped to make our Sports Day a great success!" The headmaster went a bit red, then laughed along with everyone else. "So it gives me great pleasure to present a special certificate to Spot Robinson!"

Spot could hardly believe his ears. *He* was going to get a certificate?

"Come here, Spot!" Matt called excitedly. "Come and get your certificate!"

Spot didn't need telling twice. He dived off Mrs Robinson's knee and raced up onto the platform.

Mr Brown bent down and patted Spot, then he gave the certificate to Matt.

"Look, Spot!" Matt knelt down and showed him the certificate.

"It says:

> *For Spot,*
> *the bravest and fastest dog we know.*
> *From all the children and teachers*
> *at Redhill Primary School.*"

Everyone cheered and clapped. Spot was so pleased and proud he couldn't even bark. This time he *did* jump up and lick Mr Brown's hand!

Mr Brown smiled and looked quite pleased.

"We'll pin it up in the kitchen, near your basket," Matt said as he gave his puppy a hug. "This really has been *Spot's* Day!"

Jenny Dale's PUPPY TALES™

Fluffy and fun, purry and huggable,
what could be better than a kitten tale?

Bob the Bouncy Kitten

Poppy the Posh Kitten

Amy's kitten, Bob, doesn't like sitting still. He leaps up curtains. He bounces round the garden. And he especially likes climbing trees. Will Bob ever stop bouncing? Amy hopes so, before he bounces into big trouble!

Popy is not just any old moggy – she's a pedigree kitten. Only the best will do for this posh pet!
But Lisa, Poppy's new owner, can't afford sparkly collars and fancy food. Will Poppy see that life can be fun without them?